THE BOXCAR CHILDREN®

CREATED BY
GERTRUDE CHANDLER WARNER

BOOK

154

MYSTERY AT CAMP SURVIVAL

ILLUSTRATED BY
ANTHONY VanARSDALE

ALBERT WHITMAN & COMPANY
CHICAGO, ILLINOIS

Copyright © 2020 by Albert Whitman & Company
First published in the United States of America
in 2020 by Albert Whitman & Company

ISBN 978-0-8075-0760-5 (hardcover)
ISBN 978-0-8075-0766-7 (paperback)
ISBN 978-0-8075-0767-4 (ebook)

THE BOXCAR CHILDREN® is a registered
trademark of Albert Whitman & Company.

Printed in the United States of America
10 9 8 7 6 5 4 3 2 1 LB 24 23 22 21 20 19

Illustrations by Anthony VanArsdale

Visit the Boxcar Children online at www.boxcarchildren.com.
For more information about Albert Whitman & Company,
visit our website at www.albertwhitman.com.

Contents

Wildman Willie

Six-year-old Benny Alden howled at the TV. He was watching his favorite show, *Wildman Willie*. The man on the show practically lived outdoors, and in each episode, someone hired him to solve a problem.

This week a wolf had been separated from its pack and was trying to hurt a farmer's chickens. The farmer had hired Wildman to take the wolf back to its pack. Wildman had tracked the animal all day. Now it was getting dark outside, but he was too close to give up.

Wildman howled like a wolf, "WhooooOOOOO."

Benny howled like a wolf, "WhooooOOOOO."

Wildman listened.

Benny listened.

In the distance, a wolf howled back. The howl was leading Wildman to the wolf's den.

Suddenly, Wildman stopped. Benny leaned closer to the TV. Wildman poked a stick into what looked like a pile of mushy rocks. "Fresh wolf scat," he whispered. "We're gettin' real close."

Benny's heart raced. He knew from the show that *scat* was another name for animal poop. Old scat turned hard. Mushy scat like this meant the wolf was nearby. Benny barely breathed as Wildman ran through the woods. He would find the wolf. Wildman Willie *always* found what he was looking for.

"Ben-ny. Oh, *Ben*-ny."

Benny didn't hear his sister calling for him. He was tracking the wolf with Wildman.

"Ben-ny. *Ben*-ny. There you are." Ten-year-old Violet stepped in front of the TV. She held a basket of laundry.

"Violet!" cried Benny. He tried to look around her. "Wildman is about to find the wolf!"

"And *we* are about to fold laundry," said Violet.

2

"I'll only move if you promise to help."

Benny nodded and tried to see the TV. Violet sighed and sat down.

"A wolf has been sneaking into a farmer's yard. It's trying to hurt the chickens," said Benny.

Violet shivered. "How awful." The T-shirt she'd been folding lay forgotten in her hands. Sister and brother watched as Wildman eased a rifle off his shoulder. Violet gasped.

"Don't worry," said Benny. "Wildman won't hurt the wolf. That rifle shoots tank...tank..."

"*Tranq*uilizer darts?" she asked.

"Yes," said Benny. "They'll make the wolf sleep so Wildman can take it back to its pack."

Wildman stopped and whispered to the camera, "There's the den. The wolf's inside."

A commercial came on. One always did just before the show's ending.

"Socks," said Violet.

Benny dug through the laundry basket, searching for all the socks. His thoughts drifted back to when he and his brother and sisters had lived in the woods.

After their parents had died, the four Alden children had run away. They'd heard they would be sent to live with a grandfather they'd never met. They thought he would be mean. At first, they had lived outside. Then one night they'd found an old railroad car. The children had turned the boxcar into a cozy home. After a while, their grandfather found them. He'd been searching everywhere for them, and it turned out he wasn't mean at all. Now they all lived together in Grandfather's house.

The commercials ended, and Wildman Willie came back on. He put a finger to his lips, reminding the people watching to stay quiet. Benny and Violet held their breath as Wildman tiptoed toward a mound of leaves. He raised his rifle. They jumped as Wildman yelled, "HUH!" A startled wolf dashed from its den. Wildman pulled the trigger. A tranquilizer dart shot into the wolf's rear end. Slowly, the wolf rolled onto its side, asleep.

"He did it! He did it!" yelled Benny.

Violet clapped her hands. "That was exciting!"

Fourteen-year-old Henry and twelve-year-old Jessie ran in. "What's all the noise?" Jessie asked.

Wildman Willie

"Wildman Willie caught the wolf," said Benny.

"Judging from all that noise, I think *you're* the wild man," said Henry, roughing his little brother's hair.

Henry and Jessie sat on the floor and helped sort laundry. Their dog, Watch, curled up on the sofa. On the TV, Wildman introduced the Show Us Your Adventure part of the show. In it, Wildman showed off photos and videos people had submitted of their own adventures in the wild. Benny really, *really* wished he could be on the show. He looked at the polka-dot sock in his hands. A video of him folding socks wouldn't be very exciting. "I miss living in the boxcar," he said. "It was so much fun."

Jessie tossed him the matching sock. She thought about reminding him that there were hard times in the boxcar too, like the time Violet had gotten sick. The children had been lucky to have help close by when that had happened. Instead, she said, "Wildman is never alone. He has a whole bunch of people along with him. You just don't see them because they are off camera."

Benny shrugged. "He still *does* all the cool stuff

5

himself. Last week he jumped into a frozen lake."

Henry chuckled. "Why would anyone do that?"

"To show people how to get out," said Benny. "I've learned all sorts of survival tricks from Wildman."

On the TV, Show Us Your Adventure ended. The scene changed to Wildman Willie lifting the sleeping wolf into his rescue plane. "I'm flying this wolf to a new home deep in the wilderness," said Wildman. "There he'll be back with his pack and won't be harming nice people's chickens." Wildman saluted the camera. Benny saluted back. "Until next time," said Wildman. "Be smart. Stay safe." He climbed into his plane and took off into the sky.

The children finished stacking the folded clothes. "Camp Survival!" boomed a voice from the TV. "Where campers survive in the wilderness just like Wildman Willie."

Benny whirled around. "Wha—?"

"Yes," boomed the deep voice, "you too can camp outdoors, forage for food, cook over campfires." The commercial showed happy children toasting marshmallows on sticks over a fire. "Camp Survival. Big Pine Lake, Maine. For children six to sixteen years of age. Register now."

"I'm six!" shouted Benny. "I could go to—"

"Lunch is ready," called a woman's voice. It was Mrs. McGregor, the Aldens' housekeeper.

"Coming!" said Henry, clicking off the TV.

Camp Survival, thought Benny. He had to remember that name. *Camp Survival. Camp Survival.* He just *had* to.

***

Mrs. McGregor bustled around the kitchen, pouring milk and setting out a platter of sandwiches. Mrs. McGregor took care of the Aldens' cooking and cleaning. She was also a close part of the Alden family.

Grandfather walked in. His blue eyes twinkled as he looked at his grandchildren. "Is there room for one more?"

"Here," said Benny, patting the chair next to him.

"Thank you, Benny," said Grandfather. "What are you eating?"

"PB and J," said Benny.

"A fine choice." Grandfather searched the platter

for another peanut butter and jelly sandwich.

"There's a..." Benny started. "There's a camp called..." But he had forgotten the name. "It's called..." He closed his eyes and thought of campers fishing and cooking and surviving on their own. "Camp Survival!" he said. "Kids live in the wild just like Wildman Willie. Can we go? Please. Please. *Please?*"

Grandfather chewed thoughtfully. "Where is this camp?"

"Big Pine Lake, Maine," said Jessie.

Something changed in Grandfather's face. "Big Pine Lake, huh?" He took another bite of sandwich. "What do the rest of you think?"

"I'd like to research Camp Survival," said Jessie. She was a whiz at finding out things online. "We'll see if they have interesting programs. If campers like going there. If the counselors are nice."

Grandfather turned to Violet. "What about you?" he asked.

"I would love to sketch life in the woods," she said. "Trees, flowers, animals. Like I did when we lived in the boxcar."

"Hmm," said Grandfather. "Henry?"

Henry speared a pickle from the jar. "I've been studying outdoor survival in Boy Scouts," he said. "It would be fun to try things I've learned."

Grandfather finished his milk. "Jessie," he said, "why don't you research the camp on the computer. I'll make some phone calls. We'll talk everything over at dinner."

"Hoo-RAY!" yelled Benny.

Grandfather held up a hand. "Hold on," he said. "It's not a yes. It's a 'we'll see.'"

All afternoon, Benny ran back and forth between Jessie's room and Grandfather's office. Jessie printed out information about the camp. They learned that the first two days would be spent learning skills. Then their skills would be put to the test on a three-day hike. Jessie also found online reviews posted by past campers. It seemed like everyone had a good time, except for one girl who got poison ivy. She posted a selfie of her face covered with a rash. "My bad," she said. "I forgot to watch where I was walking."

By dinnertime, it was settled. "Well," said

Grandfather, "it looks like the Aldens are on their way to Camp Survival."

***

A week into their summer vacation, the children dragged duffel bags up from the basement. They wrote their names on clothing tags. Jessie was racing past the kitchen with an armload of blankets when she heard Grandfather's hearty laugh. *Is he speaking with Mrs. McGregor?* she wondered.

Jessie peeked into the kitchen. Grandfather was sitting with Watch. "Yes, yes," he was saying into the phone. "He is a fine traveler. You can take him anywhere. He's young and eager—always first on and first off."

Jessie smiled. It sounded like Grandfather was talking about Benny, who always raced to be first— first to the table, first to the door, first to the car. "Oh, yes," said Grandfather. "He'll do just fine up in the air."

Jessie carried the blankets upstairs. "Up in the air?" The Aldens were driving to camp, not flying. What could "up in the air" mean? And who was Grandfather talking to in such a friendly way?

Mystery at Camp Survival

The night before the children left, they gathered in the living room to double-check their packing list. Watch rested his head on his paws. His eyes looked sad. "I'm afraid he knows we're going away," said Jessie. The children liked having Watch along on their adventures, and Watch loved being outdoors, but Camp Survival did not allow pets.

"Don't worry," said Henry. "Mrs. McGregor will give him extra treats and let him run through the sprinkler."

Violet nuzzled Watch's head. "She does spoil him when we're away."

The next morning, Mrs. McGregor and Watch waited as Henry helped Grandfather lift the duffel bags into the back of the minivan. One by one, each child hugged their sad-eyed dog.

"Time to go," called Grandfather. The children scrambled into the van. As they buckled up, Grandfather walked around to the back. He moved their duffels then closed the door. Soon they were on their way to Camp Survival.

It wasn't until they reached the highway that they found they had a stowaway.

The Long Ride

The Aldens had not gone far before Benny got squirmy. He pushed his feet into the back of Grandfather's seat. Henry knew his brother had a hard time sitting still. He needed a distraction, so Henry whirled around and rolled his eyeballs this way and that. He pushed his nose left and right, up and down. He twisted his lips every which way.

Jessie giggled. Which gave Violet the giggles. Which gave Benny the giggles. Soon, the children were seeing who could make the funniest faces, and laughing so hard their sides hurt. That's when they heard it.

Arrrr-arf. Arf, arf. Arrrr-arf, arf, arf.

Jessie spun around to look in the back of the

van. Watch's head was sticking out from the pile of duffels. *Arrrr-arf, arf, arf.* He was dog-laughing right along with them.

The children turned to Grandfather. But he kept driving as if he hadn't heard a thing.

"Grandfather," said Violet, "Watch got in the car."

"Hmm," said Grandfather. "How strange. Well, some nice fresh country air will do him good, I suppose." The children looked at one another. Grandfather didn't seem at all surprised that Watch was in the car. "Besides," Grandfather said, "he'll be good company on my ride home after I drop you at camp."

Henry took out his phone and typed in, *Driving distance from Greenfield, Connecticut, to Big Pine Lake, Maine.* "Our ride," he announced, "will take six hours."

Benny groaned. "That's so loonnnggg."

"We'll stop every hour or so," said Grandfather, "to go to the bathroom and stretch our legs."

"I'll set my phone alarm for one hour," said Henry. Henry used his cell phone all the time. He knew it was going to be hard to live without it for a whole week. But the camp didn't allow phones. Too many campers dropped them into lakes or lost them on hikes.

Violet handed out small boxes of raisins. Snacks always made a long ride go faster.

Jessie studied the Camp Survival brochures. "The first things they'll teach us," she said, "are the basics."

"Like what?" asked Benny.

"How to find shelter," said Jessie. "How to set up camp and start a fire. Things like that."

"That stuff is *easy*," said Benny. "I can't wait for the hike. Then we'll *really* be like Wildman Willie."

Violet twirled one of her braids, thinking. Wildman always made living outdoors look easy. But once, when the children were in the boxcar, they had been caught in a rainstorm. Violet had been so cold, she thought she might never feel warm again. They didn't show *those* things on TV.

As if reading Violet's mind, Jessie said, "I don't think *any* of it will be easy...But no matter what, we'll do it together."

Violet smiled. It reminded her of the book Jessie had been reading to her at night: *The Three Musketeers.* "That can be our motto," Violet said. "Just like the Musketeers. All for one..."

"And one for all!" they answered.

Violet relaxed. If she couldn't do something at Camp Survival, her brothers and sister would be there to help. And *she* would help *them.* All for one and one for all!

After a little while, Henry's alarm beeped. "Time for a break," he said, and Grandfather pulled into a rest station.

The children got out to stretch and use the bathroom. Benny ran laps around the rest area to get out all of his energy. Watch tried to join him, but Grandfather held him close with a leash.

That's strange, thought Jessie. *If Watch snuck into the minivan, how did Grandfather have a leash for him?*

But before she could ask her siblings about it, the Aldens were back on the road.

***

Five hours later, Benny cried, "Look!"

The Long Ride

A billboard said, *Camp Survival 5 Miles.*

Grandfather eased the minivan onto a narrow road. It led them deeper and deeper into the woods.

"I used to hike in woods like these," said Grandfather.

"You hiked?" asked Benny.

Grandfather chuckled. "I wasn't always old. In fact, I was once quite the athlete. My favorite place to hike was around Lake Minnehaha."

"That's a fun name to say," said Benny. "Minne—ha-ha."

"What was your favorite part, Grandfather?" Violet asked.

Grandfather thought for a moment. "I loved hiking and camping most of all," he said. "The forest is magical in the morning. Feeling the cool air on your face. Smelling the soil and plants. Listening to birds calling. Insects buzzing and clicking."

"Look!" Benny pointed to another sign: *Camp Survival 2 Miles.*

Grandfather turned onto a dirt road that seemed more pothole than road. He slowed down and drove carefully.

"What was the strangest thing you ever saw?" asked Jessie.

Grandfather steered around a deep hole in the road. "I guess the strangest thing happened one night when I was looking for a place to camp," he said. "It was nearly dark when I saw a boulder with two trees growing on top. At dusk, that rock looked like a giant moose's head with two big antlers! I just about took off running when I saw it!"

The children laughed at the thought. "Another time," said Grandfather, "I saw a tree that grew with half its trunk on one side of the trail and half on the other."

"What did you eat when you camped?" Benny asked. Benny's thoughts were never far from food.

"Mostly berries and plants I found," said Grandfather. "But once I was lucky enough to find morel mushrooms in a dried-up creek bed."

"How could mushrooms be lucky?" asked Violet.

"Because," said Grandfather, "it's tricky to find morels. There's an old saying: 'Morels are everywhere and impossible to find.'"

"Like leprechauns," said Jessie.

The Long Ride

"Or my shoes," said Benny. He sometimes wore two different shoes to school because he could find only one from each pair.

Henry said, "Some mushrooms are poisonous."

"That's right," said Grandfather. "But the morel looks unique. Some say it looks like a sponge. I think morels look the way your fingers do when you've been swimming too long—all wrinkly and puckered and pruney."

Violet scrunched her nose. "Why would anyone eat them?"

Grandfather laughed. "They taste great. Of course, over the years, I did have a few adventures that were dangerous."

The children leaned in. They wanted to hear what kind of dangers Grandfather had faced. Wolves? Bears? Porcupines?

"Once, I was hiking by myself and came across a—"

The steering wheel jerked as the van hit a deep pothole. Grandfather gripped the wheel. "Oh my," he said. "That was almost a dangerous situation itself! I'd better focus on driving."

The children hoped Grandfather would finish his story, but soon they reached Camp Survival. As the children unloaded the duffel bags, Grandfather said, "I want all of you to remember this: The trick to living in nature is to listen. Listen to what people at camp teach you. Listen to what the world around you tells you. Listen to what your instincts tell you. Do that, and you'll do great."

As the children carried their gear toward the camp, a wiry young woman jogged up with long, graceful strides. An older, bearded man followed, leaning on a carved wooden cane.

"I'm Lani," the woman said as she shook their hands. She had bright eyes, a friendly smile, and a firm handshake. "I'm Camp Survival's head guide. I'll be leading you on your hike later in the week."

The older man limped forward. He was as big as a bear. "You must be the Aldens," he said, shaking each child's hand.

"You're big" said Benny.

The man laughed a deep laugh. "And you must be Benny."

Benny's eyes grew. "You know my name?" he said.

The Long Ride

"It's my job to know what's going on at Camp Survival." The man winked. "I'm Grizzly Michaels, camp director and owner. You're in for some great adventures. I've taught my granddaughter Lani everything I know about surviving in the wilderness."

"This is our grandfather," said Henry. Henry was sure Grandfather would want to ask Grizzly some questions. Whenever the children stayed someplace, Grandfather always made sure he had the details. But this time Grandfather only nodded. "James," he said.

The big man gave a small nod and smile in return.

Suddenly, Watch ran up and put his paws on Grizzly's legs.

Jessie pulled Watch's leash. "Down, boy, down."

"Oh, he's fine," said Grizzly, rubbing Watch's head. "Hello, boy. Hello." Watch sat, wagging his tail. "Good Watch."

Grandfather glanced at the time. "It's getting late," he said. "It's too far for me to drive home tonight. I'd better find a motel."

The Long Ride

The children were surprised Grandfather was leaving so quickly. They thought he might want to see the camp, but they hugged him and Watch and said good-bye.

"Come on. I'll show you to your yurt," said Lani.

A yurt, it turned out, was like a tent. It was round on the sides and pointy on top. Inside were four cots.

"The bathrooms are in the log cabin just down the path," said Lani. "I've put canteens of fresh water next to your beds." A loud cowbell clanged in the distance. "That's the dinner bell. When you're ready, just follow the path to the biggest yurt. That's our mess hall. See you soon!"

Lani left them alone. For a moment, the children stood quietly. They'd thought about Camp Survival for so long. Now that they were there, it all felt a little strange.

"I bet Grandfather would have loved to see these yurts," said Henry. "It's too bad he had to leave so quickly."

"Did it seem like Grandfather was in a hurry to leave?" asked Violet. "He spent so much time talking about being in nature, but then he couldn't wait to get to his motel."

"Maybe he was worried about the motel filling up," said Benny.

"Maybe..." said Jessie. She had thought Grandfather was acting strange all day. "But he barely said a word to Grizzly. It's not like him to be impolite."

"That's another thing," said Henry. "Was it just me, or did Grizzly say Watch's name? How did he know what we call him?"

Benny shrugged. "It's his job to know who's coming to the camp. Remember?"

"But *we* didn't even know Watch was coming along," said Jessie.

The children thought about this for a moment. It *was* surprising. But the dinner bell reminded them they had bigger things to think about—mainly how hungry they were. The Aldens found the path to the mess hall and followed the other campers to their first meal at Camp Survival.

CHAPTER 3

Fire, Shelter, Water

A horn blared. The sleeping children bolted up in bed.

"What's that?" asked Violet.

"It sounds like a trumpet," said Jessie, rubbing her eyes.

The horn blared again. It was coming from the loudspeaker outside. Henry was the first to understand. "That's a bugler playing reveille," he said. He stretched and yawned. "It's the tune the army plays to wake up soldiers. They play it at Scout camp too."

Grizzly's deep voice boomed over the speakers, "Good morning, campers. It's a beautiful day at Camp Survival. Please report to flag-raising in

25

twenty minutes."

The children dressed quickly and joined the other campers walking toward a tall flagpole. Grizzly gripped his cane in one hand and a large folded flag in the other. Lani took the sides of the flag and clamped them onto the flagpole ropes. Everyone put a hand over their heart as Lani raised the flag.

When Lani finished, the campers rushed to the mess hall for breakfast. Benny slowed to walk with Grizzly. "Our grandfather has a big flag like that," said Benny. "A friend gave it to him. I think his friend used to be in the army."

Grizzly laughed. "Well, now, isn't that something? I'll bet he has lots of good friends. You must be very proud of your grandpa."

"We are," said Benny.

Grizzly patted Benny's head. "You'd better hurry along," he said, "before the food's all gone."

After breakfast was finished, the campers were put into groups. Today they were going to learn about the basics of survival: Fire, shelter, water. One by one, groups peeled off with counselors for their sessions. One counselor, as big as a football player, saw the Aldens and jogged over. "I'm David Shea," he said. "But everyone calls me Fireman because I'm in charge of teaching campers how to start safe fires."

"Oh, we know how to do that," said Benny. "We have lots of cookouts at home."

"Hmm," said Fireman. "How do you start your fires?"

"Well, Henry does that part," said Benny. "He uses matches."

Fireman nodded. "What would you do if you ran out of matches in the wilderness?" he asked.

Benny thought about this. Even in the boxcar, they'd been able to get matches from town.

"We could pack lots and *lots* of matches," said Benny.

"And what if you fell in a stream or got caught in a storm and the matches wouldn't light?" asked Fireman.

This time Benny did not have an answer.

"Then we would go to a hotel," said Henry. The children laughed.

"At Camp Survival, we teach you how to live in the wild without many supplies," said Fireman. "Because if an emergency does happen, you might not have the supplies you'd expect."

"Do emergencies happen a lot?" asked Violet. She loved being in nature, but she did *not* enjoy being in danger.

Fireman gave her a soft smile. "Fortunately, most people never find themselves in a survival situation. Lots of people come to our camps just to learn new skills. Others want to see what it's like to try and survive on their own. Have you ever watched a show called *Wildman Willie*?"

Benny's hand shot up. "I *always* watch it," he said.

"Well, Willie was a camper here."

"No way!" said Benny.

"Way," said Fireman. "Grizzly taught him everything he knows. Now, let's learn to build a fire."

Fireman taught the children three different ways to start a fire. The hardest was called a hand drill. It involved taking a long stick and spinning, or "drilling," it into another piece of wood. Fireman worked a long time before the piece of wood started to smoke. Each of the Aldens tried, but none of them could do it. "It takes practice," said Fireman. "But I wanted to show you it could be done."

Next, Fireman showed them something called a bow drill. It was like the hand drill, but it used a cord of string twisted around the stick to make the stick spin faster. This time, Henry was able to make a small ember. It wasn't much, but the Aldens cheered when they saw it.

Finally, Fireman pulled a metal stick from his pocket. "This is a Ferro rod. If you hit a rock or piece of metal against it, it makes sparks. Did any of you bring a pocketknife?"

"I did," said Henry. He took out the pocketknife Grandfather had given him for his birthday.

Fireman handed Henry the metal rod. "Strike it with the back of the blade," he said.

Henry did, and bright sparks flew up.

"Wow!" said Benny. "That's cool."

"If you were here for weeks, I'd have you starting fires with two sticks, no problem. But since time is short, you can use this Ferro rod. It will come in handy when the four of you are out on your own."

***

In the afternoon, the Aldens took a shelter-building class with a cheerful counselor named Alexandra. "Building shelters," said Alexandra, "is the most important thing you will learn this week. You can survive a few days without water. And a few weeks without food. But to live in the wild, you must protect yourself from rain and snow and cold."

Alexandra brought the Aldens into the woods. She taught them how to make a quick shelter by leaning large branches against a rock. Benny was the first to crawl inside. "It's cozy in here!" he called.

The children made the next shelter by heaping sticks and branches and leaves into a tent shape. This time, Benny was the only one who fit inside.

"This one is *extra* cozy," said Benny. It reminded him of the forts he built in the living room at home. He'd throw sheets and blankets over some chairs and crawl inside. It was his favorite way to watch *Wildman Willie.*

Alexandra nodded. "This is called a debris hut.

It's made for cold weather. The smaller and tighter you make it, the better it is at keeping you warm."

After the children were done with shelter-building, they headed back to camp. On the way, Benny crouched by a creek to get a drink. He was thirsty from moving sticks and branches.

"Stop!" shouted Alexandra, jogging up behind them. Her voice was sharp. "Do not drink that water."

"B...but," said Benny, "Wildman Willie drinks from the river all the time."

"That might make for good TV, but it's not a good idea in real survival situations. You don't know what's in that water. Even a clear creek can have bacteria in it that can make you sick."

"This creek looks just like the one we used to live near," said Violet. "We drank that water all the time."

"You children were lucky in that boxcar," said Alexandra. "In the wild, you should always boil your water to kill any bacteria. *Always*. Then you can be sure it's safe to drink."

Violet got a strange look on her face. She was

about to ask Alexandra a question, but Benny spoke up first.

"I'm *thirsty* though," he said.

Alexandra took a pot out of her backpack. "Then let's learn how to find and boil water the right way."

***

By bedtime, the tired children could barely keep their eyes open. But as Jessie walked down the path from the washroom, a glimmer of silver caught her eye. There was a minivan parked behind the mess hall. In the dark, it almost looked like Grandfather's. *That can't be,* thought Jessie. *Grandfather left last night.*

The other children were talking when Jessie walked into the yurt. "I'm *positive* Alexandra said 'boxcar,'" Violet was saying. "How did she know we lived in a boxcar?"

"Someone must have told her," said Henry. "No one here knows us. We learned about this camp from that *Wildman Willie* commercial."

Jessie put away her washcloth and toothbrush. "I think I saw Grandfather's minivan near the mess hall," she said. "Maybe someone drove him

and Watch to a motel. Grandfather could have told them about the boxcar then."

"That makes sense," said Henry. "The road *was* pretty bumpy in the minivan."

They turned out their lights, and the world went black. No streetlights or house lights. No computers or cell phones. Just black, black night.

As tired as she was, Jessie's thoughts would not be still. There were too many things that didn't make sense. She wished she could see her notebook to write them down. Instead, she made a list in her head:

1. *Had Grandfather brought Watch along on purpose?*
2. *How did Grizzly know Watch's name?*
3. *Did someone tell Alexandra about the boxcar?*
4. *Was their minivan parked outside?*

As Jessie lay there, she thought of one more thing. Had Fireman said they were going out on their own? What did he mean by that? Wasn't Lani going to be with them on their hike?

Jessie couldn't make sense of any of it. *Overtired*, she thought. When she couldn't sleep, Grandfather would say she was just overtired. That must be it. Nothing strange was going on at Camp Survival. Nothing at all.

CHAPTER 4

Into the Wild

On the way to breakfast the next morning, Jessie looked for Grandfather's minivan. There *was* a minivan parked at the mess hall. But it was dark green, not silver. *Silly*, she thought. It was dark last night. She had just made a mistake.

At breakfast, Grizzly announced, "Today, you'll each choose a special session. There are sign-up sheets on your tables. Blue sheets for six- and seven-year-olds. Green for eight to ten. Orange for eleven to twelve. And yellow for thirteen and up."

As they ate, the Aldens studied their sheets. "I'll take Foraging," said Henry, pouring syrup over a buttery stack of pancakes.

"What's for...for..." Benny didn't know the word.

"Here." Henry pointed to the word on the yellow paper. "*Foraging.* It means searching for food. Sort of like the way you're always looking for food in our refrigerator." The children laughed.

Jessie peeled a banana as she read her options. "Wood Carving," she decided, circling her choice. She wanted to learn to make useful objects like spoons and bowls.

Violet finished her oatmeal and circled *Knotting and Basket Weaving*.

Benny frowned at his only choice: Nature Appreciation. *Boring!* He slumped in his chair.

Henry patted him on the shoulder. "Cheer up. Remember, Grandfather told us to learn everything we could. I bet you'll learn something today that will help us on our hike. Remember, 'All for one, and one for all!'"

Lani came around, and the children handed her their sign-up sheets. But when she got to Jessie's, she handed it back. "Sorry, Jessie. Wood Carving is full."

"Already?" asked Jessie. "Can you add one more person?"

"Full up," said Lani. She pointed to another activity. "Navigating and River Fording is fun. Why don't you do that one?"

Jessie sighed. She really wanted Wood Carving. But she liked the sound of navigating, so she decided to give it a try.

After breakfast and cleanup, the children met with their groups. Henry's Foraging group followed a trail through the woods. Each camper got a booklet with photos of safe and dangerous plants. Their counselor, Arlo, pointed out plants along the trail. "This one's safe to eat," he'd say or, "This plant is poisonous."

Henry took careful notes. After an hour, Arlo said, "Let's take a tea break." He stopped at a white birch tree. A large black blob grew on its bark. "This is called a Chaga mushroom," said Arlo. "Does anyone have a knife?"

Henry jumped up. "I do," he said.

"Okay," said Arlo. "Cut off a lemon-sized chunk. Chagas are pretty hard, so take your time and be careful. The rest of you can start the fire."

Soon, a pot of water was bubbling on the fire

with the piece of Chaga inside. As it brewed, the campers talked about why they had chosen foraging. Henry talked about finding food when he'd lived in the boxcar. "I'm a Boy Scout now," he said. "I want to earn the Botany Merit Badge. The plants we study today will give me a good start."

When the tea was ready, Arlo sweetened it with honey he'd gathered from a beehive. The earthy-tasting tea provided a nice break before the group headed back into the woods. Arlo handed Henry the piece of Chaga from the pot. "Put this in your pack," he said. "You can brew it again and again. It may come in handy."

***

Benny's group wasn't boring at all. Their counselor, Hanna, taught them a fun memory game. She led them into the woods for two minutes. Then, "Stop!" she said. "What did you see?"

The campers shouted out, "Trees." "Leaves." "Sky." "Clouds."

Hanna leaned forward and whispered, "Did any of you see the rabbit hiding under a large fern?" No one had. "Did anyone see deer poop on the ground?" The group giggled at the word *poop*. But no one had seen any.

Benny raised his hand. "Wildman Willie calls poop 'scat,'" he said. "Different animals have different-shaped poop...er, scat."

"Well done, Benny," said Hanna. Benny felt proud knowing so much. "Let's walk another two minutes," she said. "Use your senses. What do you see, smell, hear, and feel?" She held up a finger. "But don't taste *anything* in the wild until you check with me. I'll tell you if it's safe to eat."

On each two-minute walk, Benny noticed more and more things. He heard leaves crunch under his shoes. He smelled pine trees. He saw fresh scat that looked exactly like Watch's poop. Benny looked around for a dog. Then he remembered Wildman Willie had said dog and wolf poop look alike. Could there be a wolf in these woods?

"Are you paying attention to everything around you?" asked Hanna. "Have you seen water? Food? Was there a place to build a fire or shelter?" The more they walked, the more they saw. "All we need now," said Hanna, "is something to taste."

Into the Wild

She led them into a clearing filled with blueberry bushes. Benny loved blueberries! "Are these safe to eat?" he asked.

"Absolutely," said Hanna.

The children picked fistfuls of sweet berries. As they ate, Hanna said, "You'll see wild blueberries everywhere in these woods. Remember the look of these leaves." She handed a blueberry bush leaf to each child. "The berries are safe to eat."

With his tummy full, Benny lay back and stared up at the sky, the clouds, the trees. *Huh? What was that?* "Hanna," Benny called. "I see something." He pointed to a black box high in a tree.

"You are an excellent detective, Benny," said Hanna. "That is a trail camera. You may see them on your hikes. They watch to be sure our campers are safe and to see what animals are around."

The children waved at the camera and made funny faces. Hanna laughed. "After lunch, I'll show you some of the photos and videos taken by these cameras. You'll see hikers and all sorts of different animals. You may even see yourselves eating blueberries."

***

Violet sat at a large worktable. The weaving counselor, Alisha, handed each camper an empty plastic water bottle. "We will be recycling these into beautiful baskets," she said. "Very carefully, use your cutting knife to take off the top of the bottle." She showed them how. Some campers needed help. But Violet, who was always making art at home, finished quickly. Then she helped the camper next to her.

"Now," said Alisha, "cut one-inch strips from the top of the bottle down to the bottom."

As Violet worked, she heard a dog bark far away. How she missed Watch. She hoped he wasn't too lonely for all of them. When she finished cutting, her bottle looked like a daisy. The bottom was the center of the flower. The plastic strips spread out from it like petals.

Alisha checked their work. "Excellent," she said. "Now, pick out your yarn to weave." Violet selected a ball of purple, her favorite color. "Watch carefully," said Alisha. She took a piece of her own green string. Starting at the middle, she wove it in and out around the petals. In and out, around and around, until the string covered the plastic petals. Alisha held up her beautiful green bowl. "Your turn," she said.

By day's end, Violet had woven a bottle basket, a reed basket, and a basket made of twigs, complete with purple ribbon. She finished so quickly that Alisha taught her several knots to use in her work as well. After class, Alisha took Violet aside. "You are a gifted artist," she said. "Perhaps, when you turn sixteen, you will return as a junior counselor and help me teach art."

***

Jessie hung upside down from a rope strung across a stream. Her Navigating and River Fording group had to cross from one side of the stream to the other. Her hands and legs were tired from gripping the rope. She heard the water rushing beneath her. A mosquito buzzed in her face. But inch by inch, she pulled her body along the rope.

The other campers cheered her on: "Keep going!" "You're almost there!" Finally, she made it to the other side and collapsed on the shore. She'd done it! She'd forded the stream. Everyone cheered. Then it was the next camper's turn.

This was the fourth stream Jessie's group had crossed. She'd learned four different ways to safely cross water. But hanging upside down was definitely the hardest. After the last camper had crossed, they picnicked on shore. One girl kept looking around. "What if bears smell our food?" she asked. "I heard they can smell food from miles away."

"Don't worry," said a redheaded girl. "This is my fourth year at Camp Survival, and I've never seen a bear. Not once."

The first girl kept looking around, just in case. A noise came from the woods. "What's that?" she cried.

"It could be a deer," said their counselor. "Or a branch falling off a tree."

The red-haired girl turned to Jessie. "The three-day hike's the best part," she said. "We all head north to Black Bear Lake. Each group goes a different way. It's fun to see who gets there first."

Jessie rubbed her sore hands. "Will we have to cross any streams?" she asked.

The girl shrugged. "I don't think so. At least, none of my groups ever had to."

Jessie was happy that she'd learned about crossing rivers, but she still wished Lani had let her take Wood Carving. Having spoons and bowls would be helpful on their hike.

***

The Aldens barely had energy to brush their teeth and shower before crawling into bed. Henry said, "Jessie, I passed by the woodworking class this afternoon. It didn't look full at all."

Jessie didn't understand. "Then why would Lani send me to Navigating and River Fording?" she asked.

Violet brushed her hair. "Maybe the class was over by the time Henry saw it," she said, "and campers had already left."

"Maybe," said Jessie. She slid under the cool covers and fluffed her pillow. Woodworking would have been so much more fun than fording streams.

The others quickly fell asleep, but Jessie's sore hands and legs kept her up. She had just started to doze when a sound jerked her awake. She got out of bed and tiptoed outside. The air was still. No sounds. No ripples on the moonlit lake. Then she heard it again. In the distance, people were shouting. A dog barked. There was more shouting, more barking.

Was that Watch's bark? Jessie would recognize her wirehaired terrier's bark anywhere.

Stop that, Jessie Alden! She hugged herself against the cold. *Stop imagining things. You did not see Grandfather's minivan last night. And you do not hear Watch barking now.* Jessie shuffled back into the yurt and fell into a restless sleep.

CHAPTER

A Journey of a Thousand Miles

It was the first day of the hike. After breakfast, the Aldens joined excited campers at the flagpole. Lani waited with them, ready to start. Grizzly wished everyone a safe trip. "Remember this proverb," he said. "A journey of a thousand miles begins with a single step."

Benny's jaw dropped. He yanked on Henry's shirt, whispering, "We're walking a thousand miles?"

"It's just an old saying," said Henry. "It means you can't get something you want unless you take the first step to get it. Like when you wanted to learn to ride a bike. You had to get on that first time. Then the next. And the next. If you'd never got on the bike, you'd never have learned to ride."

Lani led the four children around Big Pine Lake and into the forest. Their backpacks were light, with only a few days' worth of clothes and some emergency protein bars. They'd tied their sleeping bags to their packs as well. Still, Lani's backpack was twice as large as theirs were.

As the children walked, they each found a sturdy stick to help them hike the rocky trail.

Benny kept up with Lani, chattering away. He was excited to finally be on the trail. Violet and Henry came next, and Jessie followed behind. Her body still ached from crossing the river the day before. She'd barely slept all night.

After an hour, Lani called, "Rest time!" They stopped on a hill overlooking Big Pine Lake. Lani passed around a bag of what she called GORP. The children dug out handfuls of the delicious mix of granola, oats, raisins, and peanuts.

Violet took out her sketch pad and began drawing. "It's beautiful here," she said.

Lani waved her arm out across the landscape. "Camp Survival owns all of this land," she said.

A Journey of a Thousand Miles

"The camp was started nearly a hundred years ago by a man who believed all children should learn to live in nature. My grandpa Grizzly has been bringing me here my whole life. I promise, by the time your week here is over, you will love these woods as much as I do. And I always keep my promises."

Violet sketched a large log cabin on the other side of Big Pine Lake. "Whose house is that?" she asked.

"That's Grizzly's," said Lani. A yellow airplane bobbed on the water of the lake. "That floatplane is his too."

"It's like Wildman Willie's plane," Benny said.

Jessie thought back to the sounds she'd heard coming from across the lake the night before. "Does Grizzly have a dog?" she asked.

"No," Lani said. Then she seemed to think better of it. "I mean—he's talked about getting one. Maybe he did. Why?"

Jessie told her about the yelling and barking she'd heard the night before. "Oh, that's nothing," said Lani. "Sounds carry in the wilderness. What you heard was probably miles and miles away."

When they started hiking again, Jessie had trouble keeping up. Henry dropped back to walk with her. "Are you okay?" he asked.

Jessie slowed even more. She told Henry about the list of strange things she had noticed. "Could it be that Grandfather and Watch were still at the camp?" she asked.

Henry thought about this. "Maybe," he said. "Grandfather might have decided to stay instead of heading home."

"But it doesn't seem like Grandfather to change his plans without telling us," said Jessie.

Henry wiped his sleeve across the sweat on his forehead. "Maybe he didn't want to bother us," he said.

"Hey!" called Lani, far up the trail. "Are you two all right back there?"

Henry waved. "We're fine," he called. "Don't worry. We'll catch up."

Lani waved and moved on. Benny hiked next to her, pointing to something on the ground, then waving to something up in the trees. Jessie knew how much Benny had been looking forward to the hike. Grandfather would have known it too. Maybe Grandfather didn't want to be a distraction.

"You're probably right," said Jessie. "I think we can both take a lesson from Benny. Let's try to enjoy the adventure."

***

Two hours went by. When they'd first begun hiking, they'd heard other Camp Survival groups talking and laughing in the distance. But by late afternoon, those sounds had faded away. Now they heard nothing but their own voices and their shoes scraping along the rocky trail.

For a while, they sang songs. Then the trail turned steep. It was too hard to breathe and sing at the same time, so they climbed in silence, using their walking sticks like ski poles to steady themselves. From time to time, Lani stopped and pointed out a special plant or rock formation.

By late afternoon, just when the children thought they couldn't take one more step, they came to a clearing. "Look!" cried Violet, pointing to a funny-shaped boulder. Two trees grew on top,

like antlers. "That looks like the moose-head rock Grandfather told us about."

Lani tilted her head. "Hmm. I guess it sort of does look like a moose," she said. She glanced around. "This is a nice flat spot to set up camp for the night."

The children shrugged off their backpacks and collapsed on the ground. They ate pita-bread sandwiches and drank the last of their water.

"Can any of you tell me some things we need to survive?" asked Lani.

"Water," said Violet.

"Shelter," added Henry.

"Food," said Benny.

"Excellent," said Lani. She turned her canteen upside down. The last two drops dripped out. "We need water. Who remembers seeing water on our hike?"

"I do!" cried Benny. "We just passed water dripping off a rock."

"I didn't see that," said Henry.

Benny grinned. "That's because you weren't on my Nature Appreciation walk. Hanna told us to pay attention to everything. I've seen lots of things."

"Like what?" asked Jessie.

Benny took two fingers and pretended to zip his lips shut. He liked knowing things his older brother and sisters did not.

Lani said, "Violet, Benny, please fill all the canteens."

"I'll help," said Jessie.

"No," said Lani. "Benny and Violet are old enough to do this on their own. You and Henry can start the fire."

Violet and Benny grabbed the canteens and headed down the trail. Jessie and Henry gathered wood. By the time Benny and Violet returned, Henry had started a fire using the handy Ferro rod.

Lani poured all the water from the canteens into a pot. "We'll boil the water fifteen minutes to make it safe to drink," she said. "While it boils, I want you to forage for dinner."

The children stayed together. They picked only the plants Henry's book said were safe to eat. Violet's woven baskets soon overflowed with wild strawberries, raspberries, mulberries, wild carrot shoots, and radish tops. Back at the campfire, Lani had set the pot of boiled water aside to cool. The children spread out the food they had found.

"It doesn't look like enough," said Benny. He was very hungry from their long day of hiking.

Lani reached into her large backpack. "By the end of our hike, you'll be able to find plenty to eat. But since it's only the first day..." She took out a tub of peanut butter and a bag of bagels to go with dinner.

As the children ate, they all agreed everything tasted better outdoors. After dinner, Lani poured the boiled water into their canteens. "I'll go get more water to boil for the morning," she said, taking the pot down the trail. "I want you to clean up and make camp."

Jessie and Violet tied a rope between two trees and threw a piece of plastic over it for their tent. Benny and Henry leaned branches against the moose-head boulder to make a shelter. Everyone gathered dry leaves to use as mattresses.

Jessie was tightening the tent rope against a

tree when she saw something strange. "Henry," she said. He came over. "Look." She rested her hand on some green moss growing on one side of a tree. "I learned in my navigation class that moss usually grows on the *north* side of trees, where the sun doesn't shine. If this is north, that means we've been walking west all day long."

Lani walked up to them with a pot of water for boiling. "What's up?" she asked.

"We're trying to figure out if we are going in the right direction," said Henry.

"A camper told me all the groups hike *north* to Big Bear Lake," Jessie explained. "But I think we're going *west*."

Lani gave Jessie a strange look, almost as if she were proud of her for some reason. Then she turned and continued toward the firepit. "The trail always gets where the trail is going," she called over her shoulder. "We just need to follow it!"

Lani's answer wasn't an answer at all! thought Jessie. She glanced at Henry, who looked as troubled as she felt.

They turned back to Lani, who was boiling

water for the morning. She seemed so comfortable in the wilderness. Could she really be leading them the wrong way? And if so, why?

CHAPTER 6

Alone!

Benny tossed and turned in his sleep. He dreamed he was playing in the backyard with Watch. Suddenly, Watch jumped on him, pushing him into a giant pile of leaves. *CRUNCH!* "Wha—?" Benny's pillow sounded crispy. He opened his eyes. It took him a moment to remember where he was.

"Mornin', sleepyhead," called Henry. The others sat around a small campfire. "Breakfast is almost ready."

Lani set a frying pan on the fire and added some butter. From her huge backpack, she took out a plastic bottle filled with thick yellow liquid and shook it. "Scrambled eggs," she said, pouring the eggs into the hot pan. While they cooked,

Alone!

Lani passed around bagels with peanut butter. In minutes, the eggs were ready, and the children devoured their breakfast.

"Next, we break camp," said Lani. "That means leaving the place the way we found it. Henry, you'll put out the fire. Jessie and Violet, please untie your tent rope and stow the rope and plastic tarp in your backpacks. Benny, I'd like you to make sure every canteen is filled to the top. If a canteen needs more water, add some from the pot of boiled water."

The four children got to work. Soon the clearing looked exactly the way they'd found it. They rolled their sleeping bags and tied them to their backpacks. Lani checked the area. "You're good campers," she said. "I'm proud of you. Now, grab your walking sticks, and let's head out."

The trail became narrower and narrower. It grew so narrow, they had to walk single file. Benny stayed in front with Lani. Violet followed. Jessie and Henry followed in the back. Everyone had to step carefully. Weeds grew underfoot. Wild vines reached across the path.

"You can tell few hikers have walked this way," Jessie whispered to Henry. She couldn't shake the feeling Lani was leading them in the wrong direction.

Every now and then, they came to a small creek. Using their walking sticks for balance, they easily stepped across. Jessie was relieved they didn't have to ford any large streams. About an hour into the hike, they came to a clearing with an old log cabin.

"Who lives here?" asked Violet.

"It depends," said Lani. "Over the years, Camp Survival has built many cabins around the property. Most are small, like this one. But some are bigger and nicer."

"Can we go inside?" Benny asked. Lani nodded, and he turned the knob. The door squeaked open, revealing one big room with a fireplace and small window. A long wooden table and four old chairs sat in the middle. There were no beds, no kitchen, and no bathroom.

"These cabins come in handy for hikers caught in a rainstorm or blizzard," said Lani.

"It's like our boxcar," said Violet, walking around

the comfy room. "Oh!" She jumped as a chipmunk darted through her legs and out the door.

Lani ran her hand along the table. "My big sisters and I used to play in these cabins," she said. "Sometimes just the four of us. Sometimes with friends."

"You lucky duck," said Benny.

Lani smiled. "Yes," she said. "Yes, we were. Come on. We have some hard hiking ahead."

The narrow trail wound up and up and up. Every now and then, they stopped to eat a snack and drink some water. Then they'd move on. They were walking single file through a thick grove of trees when Lani suddenly held up her hand.

The children stopped. Lani put a finger to her lips and motioned them to tiptoe toward her. She pointed into the woods. At first, the children didn't see anything. Then something moved through the trees. A moose stepped out of the shadows into a ray of sunshine. It looked as big as a small car. Its mighty antlers glowed in the sunlight. For a long while, the moose stood still. Then slowly, slowly, it turned its head, staring straight at them! Benny gripped Lani's hand. *What if the moose attacks us?* he thought. *What if it doesn't want us hiking in its home?* It seemed like hours before the moose finally turned and walked away.

"Wow," said Henry.

"He was *huge*," said Jessie.

Violet's heart pounded. "His antlers were... well...they were *magnificent!*" Tonight, she would try to draw them.

"That moose looked like Grandfather's rock," said Benny, "with the funny face and big antlers."

Lani laughed. "It sort of did. But I don't think you'd want to camp under a moose."

They started walking again. This time their eyes searched the woods. They pointed out birds and toads. Violet caught sight of a red fox darting through the trees. Searching for animals made the time pass quickly. Just before noon, they came across a tree laying across their trail.

"This tree was hit by lightning," said Lani. "You can tell by this black burn mark here at the base." They moved closer to see. "It happened a while ago. All the bark has fallen off the trunk."

"Stop!" said Henry. They froze. Had he seen a snake or a wolf? Henry went off the trail and down into a dry riverbed. He bent down and reached into a clump of plants and pulled something out. "This," he said, holding up something as big as his hand, "is a morel mushroom. Like the ones Grandfather told us about." He passed it around.

"It really does look like a sponge," said Violet.

"Or wrinkly, pruney fingers," said Benny, wiggling his fingers at everyone.

"Henry," Lani said, "you're an excellent forager. I almost never find morels."

Henry squatted and studied the plants growing in the riverbed. "You have to get down and look really hard," he said. He reached down and pulled out another mushroom. "They're hiding, so be careful not to step on them."

Violet took out her woven baskets. Soon the children had filled them with morels. "I wish we had a big shopping bag," said Violet, "so we could collect more."

"Your baskets are much better," said Lani. "You wove them, which means there are spaces in them for the morel spores to escape through."

Benny looked at the baskets. Nothing seemed to be escaping. "What are spores?" he asked.

Back on the path, Lani started climbing over the trunk of the dead tree. "Have you ever planted a seed that grew into a plant?" she asked.

Violet said, "We always plant seeds in our garden back home."

The children followed Lani down the path. "Well, spores work like plant seeds," said Lani. "Except you can't really see them. There are millions of morel spores in our baskets right now."

"Millions!" said Benny. He wondered if Lani was teasing him, but she seemed serious.

"As we walk, thousands of spores are drifting out of our baskets, onto the forest floor. Some will take hold and grow. If you come to camp next year, we can look for them."

Benny looked down at his shoes. He wondered if they would sprout mushrooms too.

Ten minutes later, the Aldens reached the top of the hill they'd been climbing all day. A flat, gray cliff top stretched out in front of them. The treeless ground was as big and wide as their backyard. They stepped onto it and looked around. Below, green forest spread out as far as they could see. Hundreds of lakes and streams looked like tiny specks of blue.

Jessie looked out over the landscape. It was beautiful. It didn't seem like many people came this route. Maybe that was a good thing, she thought. After all, they had seen a moose and a fox. They'd found morel mushrooms. Were all of the campers seeing so much?

"Your hike gets easier from here," said Lani. "It's pretty much all downhill. How about we cook up these morels for lunch?"

Henry started a fire while Violet and Benny washed and dried the mushrooms. Jessie put butter in the frying pan and heated it over the fire. Henry used his knife to cut the mushrooms into big pieces and put them into the pan. The children's stomachs rumbled at the wonderful smell. Soon they were feasting on delicious morels fried in butter and sprinkled with salt and pepper.

As they finished, Lani suddenly jumped up and

ran to her backpack. She took out a walkie-talkie. Lani turned her back to the children as she talked into it.

"I didn't hear the walkie-talkie beep," Henry whispered to Jessie.

"Me neither," said Jessie.

They watched their guide talk excitedly then put the walkie-talkie away. She pulled a paper from her backpack and returned to the children.

"There's an emergency back at camp," she said. "I have to go back immediately."

"But...but, we just got here," said Benny.

Lani unfolded a large map. "The four of you will keep going." She spread the map on the ground. "See this black X? This marks the spot where you'll be picked up."

"Is that Black Bear Lake?" asked Jessie.

But Lani was putting on her backpack and didn't seem to hear. She grabbed her walking stick and turned to them. "Look," she said, "the four of you have everything you need to get where you're going. Everything. Now, I have to go." She turned and hurried back down the hill they had just climbed.

The children stared after her. Had their guide really left them alone?

"Lani?" called Violet. "Lani?"

No answer. It was just the children, the forest, and the sound of sudden wind whistling through the tops of the trees.

"Now we're really surviving!" said Benny. "Just like Wildman!"

CHAPTER 7

X Marks the Spot

Henry and Jessie could see that Violet was worried. The two older siblings were a little worried themselves, but they didn't want to show it.

"Benny's right," said Jessie. "It's part of our adventure. Remember, Violet? All for one?"

Violet smiled. "And one for all."

"The way I see it, we have two choices," said Henry. "We can continue on or go back to camp."

The Aldens gathered around the map. It was most unusual. Circles and rows of curvy lines covered the paper. Spaces were colored green or white, and there were blue lines and splotches everywhere. Most maps showed arrows pointing to the north at the top, south at the bottom, east to the right, and west to the left. But this map had no directions and no labels. The only clue they could find was the big black X Lani had drawn, showing them where to go.

"How can a map like this help us find our way?" asked Jessie.

Violet studied the map's colors. They looked familiar. She looked out over the cliff to the forest below. "This map sort of looks like that," she said. "A lot of green with some blue."

Henry snapped his fingers. "My old Boy Scout leader showed us a map like this. It's called a...a..." He closed his eyes, trying to remember. "A topographic map. It maps the shape of the land. These blue places mark water. White means the land is flat." He traced the curvy lines with his finger. "These lines show hills."

Jessie knelt over the map. "We started at Camp Survival," she said. "The camp is a flat space next to a big lake." They searched the map for blue next to white. There were many spaces like that.

"Another clue is that we've been hiking uphill," said Henry. He ran his finger along a row of curvy lines. "When these lines are far apart, it means the ground is more level. Lines drawn close together mean the ground is steep. We've been climbing some steep trails." They looked for a lake that had steep lines leading away from it.

"Here!" said Violet. "Here's a big lake with some flat land. And these lines show steep hills right next to it."

Jessie jabbed her finger at a blue line. "Here's one of the streams I crossed with my group."

The children followed the narrow lines up and up to a white spot. "This is the clearing next to the moose-head rock where we camped last night," said Henry. He moved his finger up along the line they'd walked that morning. "And here—this big white space—is the cliff top we're sitting on right now!"

"Yes!" shouted Benny. "We know where we are!" He jumped up and ran around the map, giving everyone high fives.

Violet drew an O on the map to mark their cliff. "Now," she said, "all we have to do is figure out how to get from O to X."

Henry stood and stretched. He walked to the

trail that would lead them toward the X. "If we want to keep going, this is the route to take," he said. He tilted his face up, feeling the warm rays of the late afternoon sun.

Jessie stared at Henry's shadow. It was behind him. "You're facing west!" she said. "I knew it. Lani was bringing us west this whole time."

"But..." said Violet. Her voice trembled. "I thought you said Black Bear Lake was north."

Henry saw his shadow stretched out behind him to the east. Jessie was right. They were heading west. He sighed. "I don't know where this map is taking us."

"Maybe Lani made a mistake," said Violet. "She wouldn't bring us the wrong way on purpose."

Jessie thought back to what Lani had said. "*The trail always gets where the trail is going.*" She thought about the strange way Grandfather had been acting. She was starting to think there was something bigger going on, and that Grandfather might have something to do with it.

"I have a feeling Lani knew what she was doing," said Jessie. "I think we should keep going. We can always turn back if we need to."

"WhooooOOOOO," howled Benny, just like Wildman. He ran to put on his backpack. The others stared at their little brother. They'd been so careful not to worry him. But Benny didn't seem the least bit afraid of being left alone in the wild.

Jessie lifted her backpack. A thick rope coiled on the ground underneath. Lani's rope. She must have forgotten it. Jessie strapped it to her backpack. She'd give it back to Lani the next time she saw her. *If* she saw her again.

As they started hiking, Violet said, "That *X* on the map looks far away from here. Really, *really* far away."

"Yup," said Benny, eager to start his adventure. "But Lani said the rest of our hike is all downhill. And downhill is my favorite direction!"

***

Weeds had grown over the little-used trail. Sometimes the trail disappeared altogether. Without Lani to guide them, the children quickly got better at finding the path themselves. Henry took the lead, stopping every now and then to check the map.

Benny was so busy looking for critters and insects that he fell behind. A few times, he noticed a trail camera high in a tree and waved. Benny wondered if he should tell the others about the cameras. Would they want to know that people back at Camp Survival could see them? Maybe, but Benny liked noticing things in nature and keeping them to himself.

As they hiked, the children kept an eye out for food. Now that they didn't have Lani's peanut butter and bagels, they needed to forage more food from the forest. They made sure to check plants in Henry's foraging booklet. After a little while, their baskets were filled with wild onions and asparagus. Benny found blueberry bushes, and they filled another basket. An hour later, the trail led to a low wooden bridge wedged between two huge trees. They looked around for water, but there was none.

"Why would someone build a bridge in the middle of a trail if there's no stream running under it?" asked Violet.

They climbed onto the bridge. Acorns crunched underfoot. "These are both oak trees," Henry said.

He reached out his arms. He could touch both trunks at the same time. Benny tried, but his arms were too short.

Jessie climbed off the bridge and ducked underneath it. "These aren't two trees," she called from under the bridge. "This is one tree with two trunks." They all scrambled down to look. It was true. The two trunks connected beneath the bridge.

"It's just like the tree Grandfather described!"

said Violet. "The one he saw on his hike to Lake Minnehaha." Benny giggled. He couldn't help it. The "ha-ha" in the name always made him giggle.

The children sat on the bridge. "Something strange is going on," said Jessie. "First, we saw the moose-head rock with the big tree-antlers. Then we found the morel mushrooms. And here's the tree with two trunks. These are all things Grandfather told us about."

"See," said Benny. "Lani took us this way on purpose. She took us Grandfather's way."

"That's not possible," said Violet. "Lani couldn't know what Grandfather did when he was a boy."

"I don't know how she did it, but it makes sense," said Henry. "Everything Grandfather described, we've seen."

"Remember what else Grandfather said?" asked Jessie. "'Listen to what the world around you tells you.' Somehow I think he planned for us to come this way."

It was all starting to make sense. Jessie thought back to what Grandfather had told them in the car. It all matched perfectly—the moose rock, the morels, and the double-trunk tree. She also remembered Grandfather saying he'd had a few adventures that had been dangerous. What if those were still ahead...waiting?

CHAPTER 8

A Dangerous Crossing

One of the happiest things about walking downhill was the children could sing and talk to pass the time. There was no need to save their breath the way they'd had to when hiking up steep hills.

Benny started "Row, Row, Row Your Boat." Violet followed with "Make new friends but keep the old. One is silver and the other is gold." They sang songs they'd learned at Camp Survival, including "There's a Hole in the Bucket" and "Kookaburra."

Even though they kept a lookout for animals, they never saw another moose. But once, stepping into a clearing, they came within a few yards of a baby deer. It had been drinking from a creek. It froze when it saw them. Everyone stopped. The deer was so close, they could hear it breathing. Violet stared at its beautiful eyes and sweet face. She tried to memorize every part of the deer so she could draw it later. The deer blinked once. Then again. Then it spun around and disappeared into the woods.

The path became steeper and steeper. They came to a really steep part where they had to walk sideways. "Use your walking stick," said Henry. "You don't want to lose your balance."

Suddenly, Henry's shoes slipped on loose gravel. His feet flew out from under him, and his body hit the ground hard. He was falling, falling, tumbling head over heels. Down and down. He couldn't stop.

Ahead, the path took a sharp turn. Henry aimed his body at a large bush at the bend of the path. He covered his face and head with his arms. *Crash!* His backpack slammed into the bush. He lay still.

"Henry!" yelled Jessie, edging carefully down the hill.

"Are you all right?" cried Violet.

"Can you walk?" asked Benny.

Henry didn't move.

As the Aldens caught up, Henry slowly lifted his head. He spit a leaf from his mouth. "I'm okay," he said. With great effort, he shook one arm, then the other. He stretched out one leg, then the other.

"What are you doing?" Benny asked.

"Making sure all my limbs work." Henry pushed up onto his feet.

Violet's heart was pounding fast. "You scared us," she said.

"I'm fine." Henry bent forward and rubbed his hair hard with both hands. Dirt and gravel fell out. Benny helped pick out twigs and leaves. "Thanks, Sport," said Henry.

"I guess just because the trail goes downhill," said Jessie, "doesn't mean it's always going to be easy." She brushed leaves and dirt off Henry's backpack.

Violet brought out a wipe from their first aid kit. She cleaned the scratches on Henry's hands and neck. Henry looked at his family. This is how it was when they lived in the boxcar. Caring for each other. Helping each other. "All for one," he said softly.

A Dangerous Crossing

"And one for all," they said.

"How much longer do we walk downhill like this?" Violet asked.

Henry unfolded the map. He pointed to a group of lines drawn very close together. "See this steep hill? This is exactly where we are. And here"—he pointed to a blue line—"is some sort of water."

"It looks like we're almost there," said Violet.

"It also looks..." Jessie paused. "It looks like that water runs right across our path."

***

Minutes later, the four children stood on the bank of the river. "Are you sure we have to cross?" asked Jessie. "Isn't there a way to walk around it? Or a bridge to cross over?"

"I checked," said Henry. "The only way for us to reach the X is to cross this river."

Jessie's body still hurt from her river crossing class. *You have to do this*, she told herself. *You're the only one who knows how to ford a river safely.* She thought about what she had learned. It had been hard for her to cross a river hanging upside down from a rope. There was no way Benny or Violet could do that. Luckily, the counselor had taught them other ways to cross rivers. "Hold on," said Jessie. She picked up a stick and threw it far out into the middle of the river. Then she began to walk along the shore, watching as the stick floated downstream.

"What's she doing?" asked Benny.

"I have no idea," said Henry.

Jessie kept walking. She needed to find out how fast the current was. CRACK! Jessie whirled around. Something big had moved in the bushes. A bear? The red-haired girl had said there were no bears on the way to Black Bear Lake. But this wasn't that path. Jessie looked but couldn't see anything. Still, the last thing they needed was to meet a bear. She turned and ran back to the others.

"Okay," said Jessie, "I was able to walk faster than the stick was moving. That means this water isn't flowing too fast. This is a safe place to cross." She walked to a tall tree on the shore. "Violet, what's the strongest knot you learned to tie in weaving class?"

Violet thought a moment. "The bowline," she said.

Jessie took off her backpack and unhooked the

rope Lani had left behind. "I need you to tie one end around this tree, then teach me the knot."

Violet tied the bowline three times, until Jessie understood how to make it. The fourth time, Violet made the knot nice and tight. Jessie put on her backpack, picked up the rope and her walking stick, and stepped into the river. "I'll cross first," she said. "I'll tie the rope to a tree on the other side. Then each of you can hold on to it as you cross."

Jessie stepped into the river. The cold water covered her shoes, then her socks, then her ankles. Her counselor had said to wear shoes during water crossings, in case they stepped on something sharp. She had also said it was dangerous to cross water that went above the knee.

Jessie could barely make out the river bottom. At any moment, she could step into a deep hole or stumble on a big rock. Her heart raced as she felt her way, poking the rocky bottom with her walking stick.

Halfway across, the water came up high on her calves. If it got to her knees, she'd have to turn back. They'd need a shallower place to cross. She held her breath—poking, prodding, testing the depth of the water. Little by little, the water became shallower. Soon she climbed onto the other shore.

"Yeah!" cheered the others. Henry whistled. Jessie grinned and took a deep bow. She found a tree and quickly knotted the other end of the rope around it. The rope stretched nice and tight from one shore to the other. "Okay," she called. "Just hold on to the rope and walk across. Take your time."

"You go first," Henry told Violet. "Then Benny. Then I'll go last, so I can untie the rope and bring it with me. Stay close together, and hold tight." Henry took Benny's backpack to keep it dry.

Violet had watched Jessie very carefully. She walked *exactly* the same path Jessie had. Benny held on to the rope with both hands. He slid his feet side to side, sliding his hands along the rope as he went.

They were halfway across when Violet saw it— upriver, a dead tree floated around the bend. It was coming right at them. "Look," she cried. The tree could crash into them. It could tear the rope. It could push them downstream.

A Dangerous Crossing

"Go!" shouted Henry. "Go, go, *go!*" Violet tried to hurry. It was hard to push her legs against the force of the water. In the commotion, Benny turned to look upriver. When he saw the tree, he tried to run, but he lifted his feet too high and lost his footing. Benny clung to the rope to keep from being swept downstream. Water splashed in his face. The tree floated closer and closer. Its branches seemed to be reaching for him.

Henry got there first. He scooped Benny up and raced to the other side. Seconds later, the tree rammed into their rope and tore it loose. The children stared. They shivered from cold, from fear, and from relief. Henry ruffled Benny's hair. "Well, Sport," he said. "You wanted adventure? You got adventure."

"That...was..." Benny's teeth chattered. "Awesome!"

Night was coming. They needed to make camp quickly. The Aldens jumped into action. Jessie started making shelter, Violet foraged for food, and Benny searched for sticks so Henry could start a fire. There was just one problem.

A Dangerous Crossing

"My Ferro rod!" said Henry. He felt his pockets, but it was nowhere to be found. "It must have fallen out when we were crossing the river."

"How will we start a fire?" asked Violet.

The air was cooling down. Even with shelter, the wet children would need a fire.

Henry grabbed one of the straight sticks Benny had collected and thought back to Fireman's class. He cut off a piece of the frayed rope to make his bow drill. Then he used the rope to spin the stick into a flat piece of wood.

Jessie, Violet, and Benny huddled close to block the wind as Henry spun the bow drill. *Back and forth. Back and forth.* After several minutes, Benny smelled something burning. *Back and forth. Back and forth.* Violet saw a wisp of smoke. *Back and forth. Back and forth.* Jessie noticed an ember. They had done it!

Before long, the Aldens were warm and cozy around their campfire, eating mushrooms and berries Violet had foraged. Henry made some Chaga tea with honey to help warm them.

"I think you earned that merit badge," Jessie

told her brother.

Henry took a sip of tea. "I think we *all* did enough to earn merit badges," he said. "Without you and Violet, we wouldn't have been able to cross the river."

Benny made a sad face. He felt left out.

"Benny, we couldn't have done it without you," said Henry. "You were our fearless leader."

"That's right, Benny. You never seemed scared at all," said Violet. "How come?"

Benny smiled. He felt it was finally time to tell his siblings what he'd learned in Nature Appreciation class. He pointed up to a tree and waved.

Jessie smiled. "Why are you waving at the tree?" She'd thought Benny had been waving at squirrels or rabbits during their journey. But now she didn't see any animals.

"I'm waving at the camera," said Benny.

Jessie laughed. She thought Benny was being funny. But when she looked where Benny was pointing, she saw a black box high in a tree.

"That's a trail camera," he said. "There are cameras on all of the Camp Survival trails. They help make sure campers are safe."

Henry and Jessie looked at each other in awe.

"They showed us in my Nature Appreciation class," said Benny. "There are cameras along every trail. That's how I knew Lani was leading us the right way. They've been watching us since we left camp."

Jessie and Henry couldn't help but laugh. All this time, they had been worried that Benny might get scared if they told him they were going in the wrong direction. But he was the one who knew better all along.

It seemed more and more like Lani's last words to them were true after all. They *did* have everything they needed to get where they were going.

The only question left was what would be waiting for them when they got there.

CHAPTER 9

The Trail to...Nowhere?

Henry crept out of his shelter and into the dim dawn light. He used his flashlight to see where he was going. Quickly, he gathered what he needed.

By the time the others woke, Henry had set out breakfast around a crackling campfire. They enjoyed a feast of Camp Survival protein bars and the rest of the blueberries they'd picked the day before. A pot of Chaga tea simmered on the fire. "I boiled water and refilled our canteens," Henry told them. "We'll have enough to get us to that X on our map."

"We still don't know where we're going," said Violet, stirring honey into her tea. "Or why."

Jessie unwrapped a second protein bar. "Lani

said we would be picked up at the X. So X is where we have to go."

The morning forest felt still around them. Slowly, the air filled with the sounds of birds calling and insects clicking and chirping. The children smelled the rich soil, the lush plants, and the burning wood. "It *is* magical here," said Violet, "just the way Grandfather said."

Benny looked at the sky. "What's that?"

"What's what?" asked Henry.

Benny cocked his head. "I hear an airplane."

As soon as he said it, everyone heard the low hum far in the distance. It came closer and closer, louder and louder. Tall trees blocked their view of the sky. Suddenly, a bright yellow plane roared overhead. It had floats instead of wheels.

"That looks like Grizzly's plane," said Jessie.

Violet hugged her knees to her chest. "Maybe it has something to do with the emergency Lani was called back for. I hope no one is hurt."

"We should get going," said Henry. "We have a long hike today." They quickly broke camp, leaving the campsite as clean as they'd found it.

The Trail to...Nowhere?

***

The map led the children away from the river. Henry kept them on the path leading to the X. Whenever one of them spotted a trail camera, they all waved. Then they made their funniest faces and did silly dances. The children wished they could see the looks on their counselors' faces, watching the monitors back at camp.

The hills on this climb were not as steep or as dangerous as the ones the day before. This trail held different surprises. Once, they came upon an open field filled with colorful wildflowers. Butterflies fluttered through the sunlight from flower to flower.

"Let's plant a butterfly garden when we get home," said Jessie. "One of the campers said she has one. She told me the kinds of flowers to plant, so butterflies come and stay."

"I'll plant a Wildman Willie garden," said Benny. "Then Wildman Willie will come and stay."

Henry laughed. "Little brother," he said, "you have some very interesting ideas." He checked the map. "We don't have far to go."

They finally reached the spot where Lani had drawn the X. It was just more trees and more trail.

"What a rip-off," said Benny.

Jessie's shoulders slumped. "What do we do now?"

Henry folded his arms across his chest. He shook his head slowly from side to side, the way he did when he was thinking. They waited. He would share his idea when he was ready. Finally, he said, "This map doesn't give exact directions. But so far, the map and the trail have led us past all of Grandfather's favorite places. That can't be a coincidence. We have to trust that we have done everything right so far. X has to be nearby."

They looked around. Trees surrounded them in every direction. Violet said, "What if we each took fifty steps in different directions? Maybe we'll find a clue to show us the right way to go."

They headed out. Each child walked to the north, south, east, or west. After fifty paces, they stopped. No one saw anything. "Let's go another fifty paces," called Henry. They walked even farther away from each other. None of them found a single clue. "Another fifty," yelled Henry. They were far apart now, but the sound carried clearly through the woods. Even after the next fifty, Henry, Jessie, and Violet found nothing.

"I found it!" shouted Benny, far from his siblings. "I found the X on the map!"

They raced toward his voice. Had he found another trail? A strange rock? Hidden mushrooms? They ran right out of the woods, onto the beach of a large lake. Benny stood grinning under a sign. He was still learning to read, but he recognized the letters of the last word: *Welcome to Lake Minnehaha*.

The Aldens whooped and high-fived. Benny had found the clearest clue of all. Lake Minnehaha— the lake from Grandfather's stories.

"We were right!" said Jessie. "We were going on Grandfather's hike the whole time!"

"That's why Lani was acting so strange," said Violet. "She didn't want to spoil the surprise!"

"What now?" asked Henry. They looked around. No one was there to pick them up. No car, no boat, no counselor, no guide.

Then Benny heard it.

CHAPTER 10

Secrets from the Past

At first Benny thought it was a mosquito buzzing in his ear. Then he saw a tiny dot in the sky. A tiny *yellow* dot.

The hum of an engine grew louder and louder. The children covered their ears against the noise. The plane flew across the water, heading right toward them. Benny's heart raced. The children scrambled back to the trees, and Benny ducked behind Henry. Still a little way out, the engine slowed. The plane flew lower and slower and closer. Finally, it splashed down and skipped across the water. The tips of the floats ran right up on shore— exactly where the children had been standing. The engine stopped. The world went silent.

Secrets from the Past

Benny peeked out. He'd never seen a floatplane up close. "That's like Wildman Willie's plane," he whispered. Benny had always dreamed of flying next to Wildman on one of his adventures.

The pilot's door swung open. "Helloooo," boomed a familiar voice. Grizzly leaned out, smiling and waving. "Anyone want a ride?"

"Me!" shouted Benny. He ran to the plane, and the others followed.

"How did you know we'd be here?" asked Henry.

"Ah, remember?" said Grizzly. "It's my job to know what's going on at Camp Survival. But I suppose you have many more questions. And I am not the best person to answer those. But I can take you to someone who can. Hop aboard."

The girls and Henry climbed into the back of the plane. Benny hopped into the seat next to Grizzly. "Buckle up," said Grizzly. The plane took off. "Want to see where you've been?" Grizzly flew them all along the trails they had hiked.

"Flying is a lot faster than hiking," Benny shouted over the noise of the engine.

Grizzly circled back to Lake Minnehaha. "I used

to come to this lake when I was a boy," he shouted.

"So did Grandfather!" Henry shouted.

Grizzly laughed. "I've heard." Grizzly tilted the plane over the lake. "When I got out of the army," he said, "I came back and bought Camp Survival." He circled lower and slower. "Of course, back then, it was called Camp White Feather." He landed in the water and taxied to a dock in front of a large cabin. A man and dog stood on the pier, waiting.

"Grandfather!" shouted Benny, pointing. "And Watch!"

Grandfather tied the plane to the dock. He opened their door, laughing. "Oh, how I wish you could see your faces," he said. "It's not often I can surprise the four of you." The children stepped onto the floats and jumped down to the dock.

Arrrr-arf. Arf, arf. Watch darted from one child to the next, tail wagging, body wiggling, jumping, and licking their faces nonstop. No one moved, for fear the excited dog would push them right off the dock and into the water.

"I don't understand," said Violet. "Have you and Watch been at Camp Survival the whole time?"

"We have," said Grandfather. "We were staying with Grizzly."

"So, that *was* your minivan I saw at camp," said Jessie.

Grandfather nodded. "Yes, I needed to stop by the kitchen to pick up some food for Watch, so I drove over. I thought you all would be in bed!"

"And that *was* you and Grizzly I heard shouting that night," said Jessie. "And Watch I heard barking."

"That's right," said Grandfather. "Another unexpected turn of events, I'm afraid. We were sitting on Grizzly's porch when Watch took off after a skunk. We yelled for him to stop. Skunk spray is one smell you don't want around you or your dog."

Grizzly raised an eyebrow at Watch. "You found out the hard way," he said. "Didn't you, boy?" Watch buried his face in his paws. "Oh, how he howled when that skunk sprayed him. Took us a long time to wash off the smell."

A cowbell rang up at the cabin. A slender young woman was there, carrying a tray of lemonade to a picnic table. Violet squinted. "Is that Lani?" she asked. "But...she said there was an emergency..."

"How about we all settle in for a nice cold drink?" said Grizzly. "Your grandfather and I have some tales to tell."

***

It was the best lemonade ever. Sweet and tart. Icy cold. The children and Lani sat around the picnic table. Watch curled up at Henry's feet. The two old men settled into wooden chairs at one end of the table. Grizzly turned to Grandfather and said, "Do you want to talk, or should I?"

"Oh," said Grandfather, "I think this story needs two of us to tell it."

"But...but," said Violet, "it didn't seem like you two liked each other."

"Part of our plan," said Grizzly. "Part of our plan."

"We wanted everything to be a surprise," said Grandfather. "And from the looks on your faces when you stepped off the plane, I think we did an okay job."

Grizzly ran his cold glass of lemonade across his forehead. "Your grandfather and I have known each other since we were twelve," he said.

"We met at Camp White Feather," said Grandfather.

"Your grandfather was a city kid from Connecticut," said Grizzly. "And I was a country boy from Virginia. We had nothing in common."

"We were opposites," said Grandfather.

"Sweet and sour," said Grizzly.

"Big and small."

"Hot and cold."

The children's heads swung back and forth as the two men played the word game. It seemed they'd played the game many times before. Grizzly stopped. "I guess we should get on with our story."

Grandfather sipped his lemonade. "For some reason," he said, "the two of us hit it off. Grizzly knew everything about the great outdoors."

"I taught your grandfather how to climb his first tree," said Grizzly.

"And I taught Grizzly how to play chess."

"One of the greatest games ever invented," said Grizzly. He looked at Grandfather. "Those six summers we spent here were six of the best summers of our lives."

Henry chugged the last of his lemonade. "If you knew each other all these years," he said, "why didn't we ever hear Grizzly's name?"

Both men looked a little sad. "When we turned nineteen, we stopped coming to camp. Our lives took different paths." Grandfather shrugged. "Back then, there were no computers to send emails. Phone calls were expensive. So we wrote letters back and forth a couple of times a year. Once, Grizzly wrote about buying our old camp. But I never thought much about it."

Benny brightened. "Until I heard about Camp Survival on the *Wildman Willie* show!" he said.

Grandfather nodded. "I didn't know Grizzly had changed the camp's name. But when you said the camp was on Big Pine Lake, I knew it had to be his. I called Grizzly that same day. We planned out the whole trip."

"So Grizzly is the friend I heard you talking to on the phone," said Jessie. "When you said someone would do just fine up in the air...did you mean Watch?"

"That's right," said Grandfather. "I told Grizzly all about your adventures in the boxcar. And I told him about Watch too."

"You see, I lost my dog a few months ago," said Grizzly. "I missed having one around, so I asked if your grandfather would bring Watch along."

"And you told the counselors about us too, didn't you?" asked Jessie.

Grizzly nodded. "Yes, that might have been a mistake. Alexandra told me she let the beans slip about the boxcar during your training."

Benny's stomach rumbled. Grizzly looked around. "Was that thunder?"

"Noooo," said Benny. "I'm hungry."

Grizzly winked at Lani. "Do we have anything to eat?" he asked. "Maybe some old prunes or stale peanuts?"

"I think so," she said. "In fact, I've set out a little something inside."

Lani's "little something" turned out to be a giant spread of hamburgers, hot dogs, salad, fruit, and desserts. The hungry children filled their plates. "How did you have time to get this ready?" asked

Jessie. "What happened to your emergency?"

"Ah, my emergency," said Lani. She waved her hand over the food. "You're looking at it. Grizzly wanted me to hike ahead and get everything ready for you. I had a lot of cooking and cleaning to do."

Jessie thought about how scary it was for them to cross the river alone. "Weren't you worried about us?" she asked.

"Not for a second," said Lani. She passed Benny the potato salad. "You had all you needed. Your grandfather was watching you on the trail cameras. And I sneaked back to make sure you all got across the river safely."

"I *knew* I heard something moving in the bushes!" said Jessie. "And that rope we used to cross the river? You left it behind on purpose."

"And Grizzly flew over our campsite to be sure we were okay!" Benny said.

"Boy," said Lani, "your grandfather told us you were good at solving mysteries. You kids don't miss a thing!"

After lunch, their bellies full, they settled into the large living room. Living outdoors was fun, but it felt good to collapse onto sofas and chairs. Grizzly went over and tinkered with the large TV. Jessie seemed thoughtful. "Benny," she said, "did you mind that there were trail cameras watching out for us?"

"No," said Benny. "We still did everything ourselves. We had real adventures. Just like Wildman Willie."

"Speaking of Willie," said Grizzly. "He was one of my star campers. He's still like a son to me. In fact, I talked to him just last night." Grizzly clicked the remote control, and *Wildman Willie* came on. "I recorded the latest episode for you," he said. "I think you'll find one part particularly interesting."

On screen, Wildman faced the camera. "This week's Show Us Your Adventure is one of the most exciting I've ever seen," he said. "So hang on to your hats. It's going to be a wild ride!"

The TV picture changed to a video of a river. Soft music played. A rope stretched across the water. A girl stood on the far shore. Three other children gripped the rope as they crossed the river.

"That's us!" yelled Benny. "That's us!"

Secrets from the Past

The Aldens clutched each other's hands as they watched. How could this be? In the video, a dead tree floated down the river into view. The music turned scary. They held their breath as the tree floated closer and closer to where the children were crossing. Benny jumped up from his spot in front of the TV and yelled, "Hurry! Hurry!"

The tree moved faster and faster. Exciting music played as the tree nearly rammed into them. At the last moment, Jessie pulled Violet to safety. Henry grabbed Benny and lunged toward the shore. The tree crashed through the rope and disappeared downstream. The exciting music faded away.

"Whew," said Wildman Willie. "How's *that* for exciting? Congratulations on a job well-done to the Alden family from Greenfield, Connecticut."

The children jumped up, clapping and cheering. "All for one," they yelled, "and one for all!"

They replayed the scene over and over again before turning off the television. Then, one by one, as they relaxed in the comfy living room, the exhausted campers drifted off to sleep.

As Benny's eyes closed, he imagined he was

Wildman Benny, saluting the camera. "Until next time," he mumbled. "Be smart. Stay safe." He climbed into the pilot's seat and started the engine. "Until next time," he mumbled.

And there would be a next time. And a next. And a next. And a next.

Turn the page to read a
sneak preview of

THE MYSTERY OF
THE FORGOTTEN
FAMILY

the new
Boxcar Children mystery!

The bright summer sun shone warmly on the four Alden children. Henry, Jessie, Violet, and Benny stood in front of an antique shop on Main Street, looking at a sign on the door.

"'Come...in...'" Benny said slowly. He was six and still learning to read. "Mul...Muldaur's Shop has re...re...'"

"'Reopened for business,'" said ten-year-old Violet, finishing the sentence.

Benny squinted at the sign. "Reopened? Do you think that means somebody else is here instead of Mr. Muldaur?"

The Aldens had been to Muldaur's Antique Shop a few times, and each time the shop's owner, Mr. Muldaur, had been in a bad mood. The last time the children had visited, Mr. Muldaur had gotten upset at Benny for petting the dog that often hung out in the shop.

"Look here," said Violet. She pointed to some small writing on the bottom of the sign: "'Muldaur's Antique Shop was closed last week due to illness. We apologize for any problems this has caused our customers.'"

"It sounds like Mr. Muldaur was out sick," Jessie said. "I'm sure he's back now."

Benny frowned. Although he did not want Mr. Muldaur to be sick, he did not want to be yelled at again either. "I think I'll stay out here and watch our bikes," Benny said.

Henry and Jessie gave each other a look. They knew why Benny did not want to go inside. But they couldn't leave Benny on his own. At fourteen and twelve, Henry and Jessie knew just what would change Benny's mind.

"Suit yourself, Benny," Jessie said. "That will leave more toys for me to find."

Benny looked up. "Toys?"

Henry nodded. "That's right. And hidden treasures for me. Who knows what kinds of things we can find to put in the boxcar."

Henry opened the door to the shop, and little

bells jingled on the doorframe. Slowly, Henry, Jessie, and Violet made their way into the shop.

A moment later, the door jingled again, and Benny came inside. "It's too hot outside," he said. Then he whispered. "Do you really think we'll find treasure for the boxcar?"

The Alden children loved the old boxcar that sat in their backyard. For a little while, it had been their home. After the children's parents had died, they'd run away. They had been worried their grandfather would be mean. The children found the boxcar in the forest and used it for shelter. The children had all sorts of adventures in the boxcar. They even found their dog, Watch!

After a while, Grandfather had found them. He wasn't mean at all! Grandfather brought the children to live in his big house, and he even brought the boxcar to be the children's clubhouse.

Jessie smiled at her little brother. "First we need to find Mrs. McGregor's gift," she said.

Mrs. McGregor was the Aldens' housekeeper. She was like family to the children, and her birthday was coming up. The children wanted to get her something special.

"I think it will be near the glassware," said Violet. Mrs. McGregor loved collecting antiques. She had a whole set of matching serving pieces. The only piece she was missing was a salt server, and Violet had found the perfect one on the Muldaur's Antiques website.

"What is a salt server anyway?" said Benny.

"It's a little bowl you put salt into when you serve a fancy dinner," said Violet. "It comes with a tiny spoon too."

Benny thought that sounded boring. But he was excited to look at all of the items in the crowded shop. The room was filled with shelves and shelves of old objects, large and small. There were lamps, books, toys, jewelry, framed pictures, and clocks. There were bird cages, musical instruments, dolls, hats, and umbrellas. There seemed to be too many things to name or count.

Violet found shelves with silver plates and other serving pieces. "I think I see it!" she said. She walked over and took down a tiny, oval bowl with a lid. An equally tiny silver spoon was nestled inside.

"Mrs. McGregor's salt server!" said Violet. "I'm glad it's still here."

"Great," said Henry, taking out his wallet. "Though I don't see anyone to pay."

"Hello?" a voice called from the back of the shop. "Is someone here?"

A tall man with curly black hair came down the aisle where the Aldens were standing. Benny hid behind his older brother. He thought for sure Mr. Muldaur was going to yell at them for something.

But the shop owner spoke in a cheery voice. "Ah, there you are! What can I do for you children today?"

"Good morning, Mr. Muldaur," said Henry. "Are you feeling all right? We saw on the sign that you were sick."

Mr. Muldaur put his hand up to a white bandage wrapped around his head. "Yes, I had a bit of an accident, but I'm doing better now. Today is my first day back—just trying to get things sorted out."

A big golden retriever trotted over to the children, wagging her tail.

"Mitzy!" said Violet. She bent down. Then she stopped. "Can we pet her, Mr. Muldaur?"

"Of course you may!" said Mr. Muldaur. Then a confused look came across his face. "But how do you know her name? Do I know you children?"

For a moment, no one spoke. "We're the Aldens, Mr. Muldaur," Henry said finally. "You know us, and we know you and Mitzy too. We've been in your store a few times."

Mr. Muldaur sighed. "Is that so?" For the first time, his smile faded. "I'm afraid I've forgotten quite a bit since the accident."

"What happened?" asked Violet.

Mr. Muldaur sat down in an old rocking chair. Then he continued: "I only remember one thing from that day last week. I was climbing up my ladder to get something on a high shelf." The man shook his head. "I must have fallen because I woke up in the hospital the next morning with a terrible headache. The doctors kept me there for a three days."

"That's horrible!" said Jessie. "How did they find you?"

Mr. Muldaur reached down to pet Mitzy. "My wonderful dog saved me," he said. "I was unconscious, and Mitzy barked and barked until someone came. What a good girl, Mitzy!"

The children had never seen Mr. Muldaur so happy before. "You seem...different," said Henry. "Are you sure you're ready to come back to work?"

"I feel great!" said Mr. Muldaur. "It's just my memory...The doctors told me it would return, but they don't know how long it will take. I can't seem to make much sense out of anything in my store."

"You did know an awful lot about your antiques," said Jessie. She thought back to the times they had visited the shop. It always seemed like Mr. Muldaur had a story for every little thing.

Mr. Muldaur smiled as he looked all around his shop. "And I remember that it's my job to know about all these things," he said. "That's what people in the antique business do. We learn about each item so we can tell customers where, when, and how it was made. We try to learn about the journey each item has taken, from its being made, all the way to this store."

"Do you remember any stories about this?" asked Violet. She held out the salt server.

Mr. Muldaur sighed and shook his head. "I'm sorry. I don't. But maybe I'll have a story soon," he said.

Benny had found the toy area and came back with an old mechanical windup bear. "What do you mean about journeys? Did this bear march here?"

Mr. Muldaur chuckled. "That would be a very interesting journey indeed!" Mr. Muldaur took the bear in his hands. "I am talking about a different kind of journey. This might have been passed down from one family member to another, over many years. Or it might have gone from child to child, crossing the country, maybe even the world! I'm sure this bear has had a very interesting journey... It's part of what makes it special."

Mr. Muldaur turned the bear on its side. He began winding it up with the key that stuck out from the side.

"Could this bear be really old, then?" asked Benny. "Like, even older than Grandfather?"

Mr. Muldaur laughed. "Yes, it may be, though

I don't remember your grandfather, or any stories about the bear anymore." He set the bear down on a table, where it slowly walked along on all fours, moving its head from side to side. Benny laughed as he watched the bear lumber ahead.

"Well, you do know our grandfather," said Violet. "Maybe when you meet him, you'll remember him."

"I sure hope so," said Mr. Muldaur. "And I hope my memory hurries up and comes back. If not, I won't be very helpful in selling these wonderful antiques."

The Alden children looked at one another. When they had first come into the shop, they had wanted to get in and out as quickly as possible. But they could tell Mr. Muldaur needed help. Jessie and Henry nodded at each other.

"Maybe we can help you get organized," said Jessie. "Until your memory comes back."

Mr. Muldaur was surprised. "Are you sure?" he asked.

"Yes!" said Benny. "We're good at finding out secrets!" The thought of hidden treasures and old secrets made him forget all about the last time he had visited the shop.

"All right, come with me," said Mr. Muldaur, standing up. "Into my 'secret office.'"

He led the children behind a bookcase in the back of the shop. There was small room with a huge wooden desk, which was buried under an equally huge pile of papers. There were more stacks of paper scattered on shelves. Open filing cabinets stood against the walls, stuffed with even more loose paper.

"It isn't really a secret office," said Mr. Muldaur. "It's more of a secret pile of paper." He chuckled. "I'm sure I wrote everything down. But I have no idea which papers belong to which items. Everything is all jumbled up. Sort of how my mind feels these days."

Mr. Muldaur looked up with a glint in his eye. "Still," he said, "I'm happy to feel better and to be back with my shop and my dog. And, I've met you four! This must be my lucky day."

"You're meeting us again!" said Benny. "And it's double lucky. We're on summer vacation. We can help you a lot."

Check out the Boxcar Children Interactive Mysteries!

Have you ever wanted to help the Aldens crack a case? Now you can with these interactive, choose-your-path-style mysteries!

GERTRUDE CHANDLER WARNER discovered when she was teaching that many readers who like an exciting story could find no books that were both easy and fun to read. She decided to try to meet this need, and her first book, *The Boxcar Children*, quickly proved she had succeeded.

Miss Warner drew on her own experiences to write the mystery. As a child she spent hours watching trains go by on the tracks opposite her family home. She often dreamed about what it would be like to set up housekeeping in a caboose or freight car—the situation the Alden children find themselves in.

While the mystery element is central to each of Miss Warner's books, she never thought of them as strictly juvenile mysteries. She liked to stress the Aldens' independence and resourcefulness and their solid New England devotion to using up and making do. The Aldens go about most of their adventures with as little adult supervision as possible—something else that delights young readers.

Miss Warner lived in Putnam, Connecticut, until her death in 1979. During her lifetime, she received hundreds of letters from girls and boys telling her how much they liked her books.